The Grimpots

Can you find the seahorse?
There's one hiding in every picture.

Diolch yn fawr i Dai, Mafys ac Elwyn

First impression: 2019

© Copyright Gilly John and Y Lolfa Cyf., 2019

The contents of this book are subject to copyright, and may not be
reproduced by any means, mechanical or electronic, without the prior,
written consent of the publishers.

Illustrations: Janet Samuel

ISBN: 978 1 78461 696 0

Published and printed in Wales on paper from well-maintained forests
by Y Lolfa Cyf., Talybont, Ceredigion, SY24 5HE

website www.ylolfa.com
e-mail ylolfa@ylolfa.com
tel 01970 832 304
fax 832

The Grimpots

Written by Gilly John

Illustrated by Janet Samuel

yLolfa

Far beneath the pea green waves,
Deeper still, are grimpots' caves.
Hidden in the salty swell
Is where the little grimpots dwell.

Mama, Papa and little Gus
Are all umbrella octopus.
With tentacles as wide as a brolly,
They're always wet but very jolly.

One day, poor Gus was swept away,
He found himself in Barnacle Bay.
He played for a while in an old shipwreck,
Until a shadow crossed the deck.

A shady shark, a fearsome fish,
Thinks grimpot makes a tasty dish.
"Little grimpot, in the reef,
You'll make a nice aperitif."

"Just a joke, we should be friends.
Tell me how to make amends?"
"Little grimpot, take the bait,
It's time to fill my dinner plate."

"Your teeth are sharp," said little Gus,
"I know that you eat octopus,
But would you like a tasty drink?"
The shark's soon lost in stinky ink.

"Ha ha," laughed Gus, "I'm very smart,
The shady shark is in the dark,
It's time that I was on my way,
I won't be grub in Barnacle Bay."

Gliding home to the grimpots' cave,
Gus met a whale, his name was Dave.
Dave bellowed loudly, "What do I see,
A little teapot, time for tea?"

"I'm not a teapot!" shouted Gus.
"I'm an umbrella octopus.
Yes, I have a waterspout,
It helps me travel in and out."

18

"Oh, what a cheery little fella,
Did you really say umbrella?
I need some shade, if you will help?
Just swim out of that green sea kelp."

19

"I have to swim above for air,
But as you see, I have no hair!
The sun has burnt my nose bright red
And steam is pouring from my head."

Without a pause, without a fuss,
"Of course I'll help," said little Gus.
Gus floated up to Dave's broad head
And settled on this strange new bed.

They gently drifted in the heat,
Laughing at the seagulls' feet.
Long forgotten, the grimpots' cave,
Sleepy Gus and big blue Dave.

Then, suddenly, the wind blew stronger,
The buoy rang out, the sound of danger.
Said little Gus, "A storm is brewing,
Too much fun is our undoing."

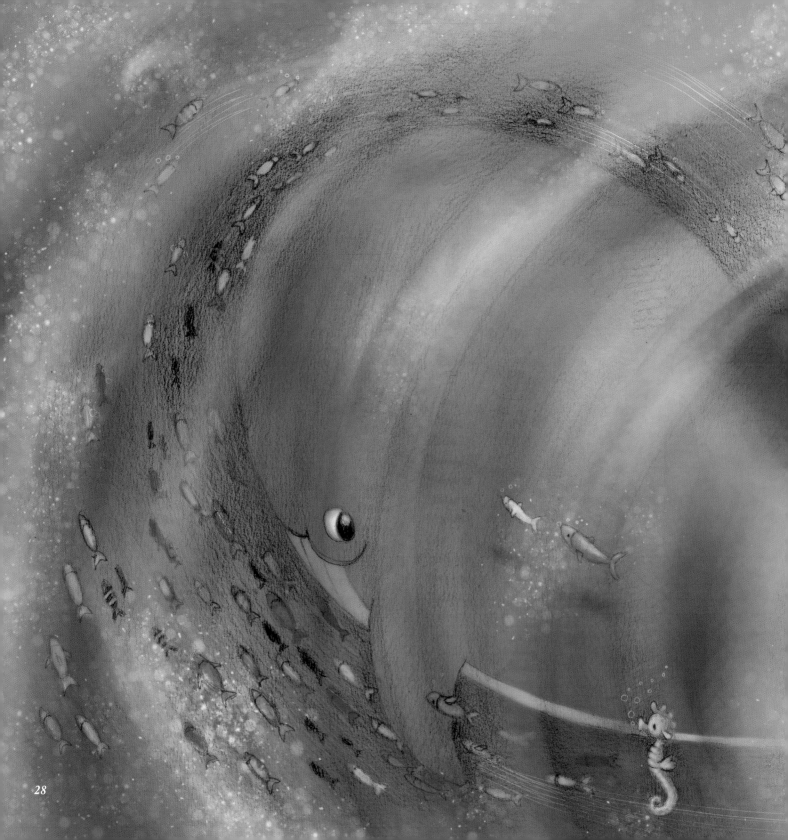

"Home time?" asked the big blue whale,
"Just hang on to my big blue tail.
But watch you don't blow inside out,
And break your little waterspout."

Fast they swam through shoals of brill,
Cuttlefish and clouds of krill.
Past pink pods of minke whale,
They plunged beneath the pale sea snail.

It all seemed such a thrilling lark,
Until appeared the shady shark.
"OH NO," cried Gus, "the shark is back,"
Will the shady shark ATTACK?

The shady shark is not so scary,
Said a starfish, "Don't be wary,
The shady shark has lost his teeth,
He left them on a coral reef."

The sea was dark, gone was the day,
Three cheers for eels that lit the way.
"Phew," said Gus, back at the cave,
"That was surely a close shave."

"Dave must stay!" said the grimpot troupe,
"There's plankton pie and seaweed soup."
"Really I shouldn't, I'm watching my weight,
But if you're quite sure, is it dinner at eight?"